Turkey

Devin Zeigler

**Other titles by Patricia Hermes
you will enjoy:**

My Secret Valentine
Something Scary
Christmas Magic

Turkey TROUBLE

Patricia Hermes

Illustrated by
John Steven Gurney

A
LITTLE APPLE
PAPERBACK

SCHOLASTIC INC.
New York Toronto London Auckland Sydney

No part of this publication may be reproduced in whole or in part, or stored in a retrieval system, or transmitted in any form or by any means, electronic, mechanical, photocopying, recording, or otherwise, without written permission of the publisher. For information regarding permission, write to Scholastic Inc., 555 Broadway, New York, NY 10012.

ISBN 0-590-50964-0

12 11 10 9 8 7 6 5 4 3 2 1   6 7 8 9/9 0 1/0

Printed in the U.S.A.   40

First Scholastic printing, October 1996

Contents

Turkey

1

No Bus

"Turkey Day, Turkey Day, Turkey, Turkey, Turkey Day!" Katie sang.

She swung her backpack around and around in front of her.

She looked down the street for the school bus.

No bus.

She was probably early. She couldn't wait to get to school, though. Mrs. Henry, her teacher, had said they were going to plan for Thanksgiving — Turkey Day, Grandpa called it. They were going to put on a program, and seven-year-old Katie Potts knew

what part she wanted. She wanted to be Pocahontas.

She smiled to herself. Pocahontas got to say a poem: "A bright and graceful child am I." Katie had been practicing it over and over to herself. She had a good chance of getting that part, too.

Mrs. Henry said everyone had to be on their best behavior for the program. Best behavior was grown-up talk for raising your hand instead of calling out in class, being on time for school, sitting up straight and tall, and not talking in line. Katie had been on her best behavior ever. Besides, she had an even better chance because she'd found her favorite lucky koala bear.

She sat down on the curb and opened her backpack. She took out lucky Koala. He was so little he could sit in the palm of her hand. He had little furry claws that clamped onto things, like the end of her pencil. She patted him with one finger, up and down his little head. "You'll help me, little Koala, won't you?" she whispered.

She made Koala nod his head.

"You'll help me get the Pocahontas part?"

Again, Koala nodded his furry head.

Katie said, " 'A bright and graceful child am I.' "

Koala nodded. He thought that was very good.

"And you'll make Obie get better soon, too, right?" she whispered to him.

Again Koala nodded.

Katie sighed. She missed her twin brother, Obie. He was sick at home with chicken pox. Her big brothers had had it, and now Obie had it.

Katie hoped she wasn't going to get it. She didn't want to get spots and itch. Obie had itched so bad last night that Daddy had had to give him a baking-soda bath in the middle of the night.

Katie leaned out and looked for the school bus again.

Still no bus.

She wished again that Obie was here. Obie was always checking his watch. He worried lots about being late.

Suddenly Katie began to worry, too. She couldn't have missed the bus, could she?

She put Koala in her pocket, then stood up and looked all around, up and down the block.

How come the other kids weren't there? Her best friend, Amelia, wasn't there, and Arthur wasn't there and Bobby Bork wasn't, and even the baby kindergarten kids — none of the regular kids were there.

Was she that early?

Or *had* she missed the bus?

She felt her heart pounding hard and a scared feeling in her stomach. She thought about what she'd done after she left the house on her way to the bus stop. She'd swung on Bobby's swing for a little while. But just a little while. She'd looked at the Thanksgiving decorations in Mrs. Anthony's window for a while. And she'd rescued a frozen worm from the sidewalk ice in front of Mrs. Moore's house.

But none of those things took that long, did they?

She sighed. Obie would have known. He'd have looked at his watch and known.

She sat down on the curb again and frowned at her shoes. For a minute, she could feel tears coming up in her eyes.

She blinked them back down. Only babies cried. Babies like Baby-Child, Katie's little brother. Or like Crybaby Tiffany.

She stood up. Should she go back home? Mom could drive her. But Mom might be mad. Mom called it dawdling. Mom hated it when Katie dawdled.

Well, she'd just have to walk, that's all. She knew the way and it wasn't that far. The big kids, like her nine-year-old brother Sam and her ten-year-old brother Matt, all walked, but little kids got to ride the bus. Mom said that was because little kids had short legs and got tired easily.

Katie wasn't tired. Besides, if the bus came along when she was walking, Mr. Barker, the driver, would stop for her. Mr. Barker was her friend.

Katie started walking. She walked up West Street to the corner. There was a stop sign there. She stopped and looked both ways. No cars.

She looked both ways again.

Still no cars.

She ran across, her backpack bumping against her.

She looked behind her for the bus. No bus. Just a few cars and a truck that had a potato chip sign on it. Katie loved potato chips.

She walked three more blocks. Three long blocks.

Now she was just around the corner from the school.

She ran the rest of the way.

The lights were on in the classrooms. All the teachers' cars were parked in the parking lot. But nobody was on the playground. Everybody was inside.

Katie looked toward the windows of the last room on the end. Her room.

She pictured Mrs. Henry and all the kids inside. What would Mrs. Henry say?

Mrs. Henry was nice about everything, everything but being late. Mrs. Henry hated that.

Katie thought about the last time she and Obie were late. Mrs. Henry had said "no recess" that day.

Katie tiptoed closer to her classroom. She stood under the windows. She couldn't see inside, but she could hear. The kids were saying the pledge. It sounded like "I pitch a lizard to the flag . . ."

She tiptoed around the corner of the building to the back door, the playground door. Maybe she could just tiptoe in and slide into her seat. Maybe no one would notice.

But then she had a really bad thought: They had to be on their best behavior to get a part in the play. And late was not best behavior.

She put a hand in her pocket and touched lucky Koala. She ran her finger up and down his furry head.

"Please," she whispered. "Don't let her notice. Please, please, please."

The Time-Out Chair

But Mrs. Henry did notice. "I'm very disappointed in you," she said.

And Katie had to sit in the time-out chair in the way back. Near yucky, blucky Tiffany.

Katie hated the time-out chair. She didn't like Tiffany much, either.

Well, she'd just have to be extra-good, that's all. Mrs. Henry would notice that she wasn't just on her best behavior — she was on her best, best behavior.

"All right, boys and girls," Mrs. Henry said. "Today I have a surprise for you. We're going to start preparations for our Thanksgiving celebration."

"The Thanksgiving program?" Tiffany called out.

She didn't raise her hand, and Katie turned and frowned at her.

Katie ALWAYS raised her hand to ask a question. Well, almost always.

"No, something different," Mrs. Henry said, smiling. "We'll talk about the program later. I thought we would have a Thanksgiving breakfast before the program. We'll make all the food ourselves. Maybe the cafeteria ladies will let us use their kitchen. We'll make the same things the Pilgrims made."

"Turkey?" Bobby Bork said.

Mrs. Henry shook her head. "No, I don't think we'll get that complicated. I thought we'd have cranberry sauce. And we could make corn muffins . . ."

"Because the Indians showed the Pilgrims how to grow corn!" Katie blurted out.

She hadn't raised her hand, and she

quickly put a hand over her mouth, but Mrs. Henry didn't seem to notice about not raising her hand.

"That's right, Katie," Mrs. Henry said. "They did."

She smiled at Katie, and right away Katie felt better. She hated it when Mrs. Henry was mad at her.

"And we could even make our own butter," Mrs. Henry said.

"Butter's bad for you," Tiffany said.

Mrs. Henry just smiled again. "You know something?" she said. "I think we're all forgetting some rules. Remember, about raising our hands?"

Everybody nodded.

Mrs. Henry smiled again. "Good, then," she said. "And we'll decorate the tables so they're really pretty. And then we'll invite our mothers or fathers or grandmothers to come. Just one parent of each child, so it won't be too crowded. And then they can stay for the program."

Katie looked over at Emil. Emil didn't

have a mother, or a father, either. He lived with his grandmother. Katie wondered if he minded not having a mother and father, and what had happened to them.

She knew Mrs. Henry had said "grandmother" for Emil.

"Do you think you'd like that, boys and girls?" Mrs. Henry said. "Making breakfast and inviting a parent or friend?"

"Yes!" a bunch of kids said together.

"I would," Katie said.

She smiled. She'd be the only one in class with both parents because Obie was in her class, too. He could invite one parent and she could invite the other.

Well, that was if Obie was better by Thanksgiving. But he would be. Thanksgiving was still a long way away.

Tiffany Bianca raised her hand.

"Yes, Tiffany?" Mrs. Henry said.

"What about the program?" Tiffany said. "I've been practicing. I could have the part of Pocahontas."

Katie put her hands on her hips. She turned and glared at Tiffany.

"We'll see," Mrs. Henry said.

"I know the poem by heart already," Tiffany said. " 'A bright and graceful child am I . . .' "

"That's nice, Tiffany," Mrs. Henry said. "But for now, let's go on with our breakfast plan."

She went to her desk and picked up some papers. "Who's the paper person this week?" she said.

Bobby Bork jumped up. "I am!" he said.

"Good," Mrs. Henry said. "Then you can hand out these papers. They're recipes for you to take home."

Bobby started up and down the aisles.

Katie turned to Tiffany. "You can't be Pocahontas," she whispered. "I'm going to be!"

"You can't," Tiffany whispered back. "Your hair is wrong."

"Wrong?" Katie said. "Yours is wrong. It's blonde."

Tiffany smiled and shrugged. "But it's straight and long," she said. "Yours is curly and not long."

"Girls?" Mrs. Henry said.

She was looking straight at Katie. "Are you paying attention?"

Katie felt her face get red.

She nodded and looked down at the paper Bobby had put in front of her.

"Now take those papers home and ask your parents if they can let you have one of the ingredients in the recipe," Mrs. Henry said.

She turned to the board and began writing things down.

"We'll make some of the words our spelling words for the week," she said. "Write these down in your spelling books."

Everybody took out their spelling books.

Katie sighed and slumped in her chair.

Spelling was her worst subject. Her very worst.

But she copied the words:

Cranberry.
Butter.
Corn.
Sugar.
Pilgrim.
Indian.

Katie could read all the words. She was a good reader. It was just remembering how they were spelled and writing them down from memory that was the hard part.

She slid a look across at Tiffany's paper.

Tiffany was writing down all the words, too. But she had written other things, too.

Katie stretched out her neck to see.

"What Pocahontas needs," Tiffany had written. And then she had checked things off. It looked like this:

Pocahontas costume – have it ✓

Pocahontas necklace – have it ✓

Pocahontas headband – have it ✓

Pocahontas moccasins – have them ✓

Katie sighed. All she had was a Pocahontas lunchbox.

But she leaned over to Tiffany and whispered, "I have all those things, too!"

Even though it was a lie. A big fat lie.

And she was very afraid that with all those good Pocahontas things, Mrs. Henry would definitely choose Tiffany.

3

Stuck Zipper

That whole day passed and the next day, and they were lining up to go home, and still Mrs. Henry hadn't given out parts for the program. Katie had been on her best, best behavior, too.

"We just got too busy these last few days," Mrs. Henry said when Tiffany asked again. "Maybe tomorrow."

"But I can be Pocahontas, right?" Tiffany said. "Please?"

Katie turned and glared at her.

"Now, hold still, Katie!" Mrs. Henry said.

Mrs. Henry was bending down, helping Katie with a stuck zipper on her jacket. Katie's zipper was always getting stuck. The lining part kept sneaking into the zipper part.

"Can I, Mrs. Henry?" Tiffany said again. "I have everything. The dress, and the moccasins, and the . . ."

"I know, Tiffany," Mrs. Henry said. She straightened up. Her face was kind of red from fighting with the zipper. And the zipper was still stuck.

"I'm sorry, Katie," she said, patting Katie on the head. "You'll just have to ask your mom to fix it when you get home. It's open enough so that you can slide the jacket off over your head."

"Mrs. Henry?" Tiffany said again.

Mrs. Henry didn't look at Tiffany. She just said, "One last thing, girls and boys. Remember to remind your moms and dads about coming to our breakfast. And ask if you can bring some Thanksgiving decorations from home."

"What kind of decorations should we bring?" Katie asked.

Mrs. Henry wiped her forehead. She still looked very hot, maybe from the zipper. She sat down on the edge of her desk.

"Anything," she said. "Anything that you might use at home for a Thanksgiving decoration. Maybe something that would look nice on our breakfast table."

"Like pumpkins?" Katie said.

"Pumpkins are for Halloween!" Tiffany said.

"Not just for Halloween!" Katie said, glaring at her again.

"I know what I'll bring!" Bobby Bork said. "My mom has baby pumpkins and teeny baby squashes. They're called hordes."

Mrs. Henry nodded and smiled at Bobby. "Gourds," she said. "They would look nice."

"I know!" Tiffany said. "Mom has dolls in costume! They're dressed up for Thanksgiving. They were in my mother's doll collection when she was a little girl. I could bring them."

Mrs. Henry smiled. "Well, ask permission first, right?"

"Oh, I will, but my mother won't mind," Tiffany said. "We have an Indian and John Alden." She twirled her long straight hair around her finger. "I'll bring in the Pocahontas things, too. They're spectacular!"

"Fine," Mrs. Henry said. She wiped her face again.

The bell rang, and the walkers started out to meet the crossing guards. After them, the bus riders went out to the bus port.

Katie walked with Amelia.

On the bus, they sat in their usual place behind Mr. Barker, the bus driver. They liked to help him, to show him where to stop and all.

When they were all seated, Katie looked across the aisle to where her brother Obie always sat with his best friend, Arthur.

Now that Obie was sick, Bobby Bork

was sitting beside Arthur. Bobby and Arthur were making paper airplanes out of their Thanksgiving recipes.

Katie wondered if Obie would get his place back when he got better.

"Know what?" Amelia said. She poked Katie.

"What?" Katie said.

"Tiffany's a pain," Amelia said. "She's going to get to be Pocahontas, I bet."

Katie nodded. "Yeah," she said. "If she brings in her spectacular costume."

"And the costume dolls, too," Amelia said.

"Who's John Older, anyway?" Katie said.

Amelia shrugged. "I think he did something big and important on Thanksgiving. I don't know what."

"Probably cooked the turkey," Katie said.

"Probably," Amelia said. "Mrs. Henry really will choose Tiffany if she brings in all that stuff."

Katie nodded. "Yeah," she said. "Know what? She's even got the headband and a necklace and a tent."

"Do you want to be Pocahontas?" Amelia asked.

Katie nodded. "Yes. You?"

Amelia nodded, too. "I don't have a costume."

"Me neither," Katie said.

"But if I can't be Pocahontas," Amelia said, "then I want you to be."

Katie smiled at Amelia. "And I'd choose you," she said. "If it couldn't be me."

But suddenly Katie had an idea. Maybe she didn't have to wait for Tiffany to bring in all her stuff. Maybe she, Katie, could come up with a plan. Tiffany's doll collection would be nothing compared to what Katie could do. With Obie's help. She and Obie were like Grandma and Grandpa. Together, they could do practically anything.

She couldn't wait to get home and get started.

4

Gobble, Gobble, Gobble

When Katie got off the bus, she ran all the way home.

She yelled hi to her mom and to Sam and Matt, who were playing on the living room floor. She patted Baby-Child, who was trying to grab a metal car out of Matt's hand. Then she pulled her jacket over her head and raced upstairs to see Obie.

He was lying on his bed, looking hot. He was playing with his new Power Ranger, a get-well present from Grandpa. Grandpa always sent a get-well present when somebody got sick.

"How are your chicken spots?" Katie asked. She plopped down on his bed.

"Bad!" Obie said. "I got more."

He pulled up his pajama top and showed her his stomach.

It looked sort of like a connect-a-dot picture.

Katie made a sad face at him. Poor Obie. He was really, really spotty. The spots were bright red, except for the black scabby ones in between.

"They still itch?" she said.

Obie nodded. He pulled down his shirt and pointed to a big red spot on his forehead. "I can't scratch it," he said. "Mom says I'll get a scar."

"You can pat it, maybe," Katie said. "That's not like scratching."

Very carefully, Obie patted his itch. "It doesn't help," he said.

"Obie," Katie said. "I need help. First, you know that rubber chicken of yours? Where is it?"

"In my toy box," Obie said.

"Can I have it?" Katie said.

"How come?" Obie said.

"For a decoration," Katie said. "I'll show you." She went over to the toy box and knelt down in front of it.

She opened it up and began dumping stuff out.

The first thing she pulled out was a rusted dump truck.

She held it up. "I remember this!" she said.

"We used it in the sandbox," Obie said.

Katie dropped it back in the box.

Next she picked up a pink, furry kitten. It had a little windup key in its stomach, and its head was sort of twisted to one side.

"Look, Obie!" Katie said.

Obie nodded. "Wallace. He used to play a lullaby. I slept with him."

"And his head wiggled while he played!" Katie said.

She turned the key.

Nothing happened. The kitten's head just lay on one side.

Katie dropped it back in the box again.

She picked up a couple of building blocks that had squiggly crayon marks all over them.

"I wonder what we made those marks for?" she said.

"Controls," Obie said. "Controls on a spaceship."

"Oh," Katie said. "I don't remember."

She dug around some more. "Here it is!" she said.

She turned around and held up the rubber chicken. She dangled it by the legs. "What do you think?" she said. "Is this a good Thanksgiving decoration?"

"A rubber chicken?" Obie said.

Katie sat back on her heels and looked at it. "Doesn't it look like a turkey?" she said.

Obie shook his head. He patted the itchy place on his forehead. "It doesn't have a wattle."

"What's a wattle?" Katie said.

"You know," Obie said. "That red thing that hangs under its chin."

Katie frowned. "Turkeys don't have chins."

"Not when they're cooked," Obie said. "They don't have heads, either. I mean before they're cooked."

Katie thought for a minute about turkey chins and turkey heads.

"Glad I'm not a turkey," she said. She bent over the toy box again. "Gobble, gobble, gobble," she muttered to herself. "Find a decoration. Gobble, gobble, gobble."

She pulled out a red felt cowboy hat. Very squashed.

She dropped it back in the box.

She sat back on her heels. She picked up the chicken again. She tried tucking its legs under it, like a turkey on a platter. The legs popped right out again. She guessed Obie was right — it didn't look much like a turkey.

"I guess it won't work," she said. She blew out a big breath. "I thought I could find something way better than what Tiffany's bringing. Her costume dolls."

"Dolls?" Obie said. "How come?"

"That breakfast I told you about? We need decorations. That's why I wanted the rubber chicken."

She held up the chicken by its legs, then dropped it back in the toy box. She sighed. "Tiffany says her dolls are spectacular."

"Tiffany's a crybaby," Obie said.

Katie smiled. Obie always took her side.

"There's something even worse," she said.

"What?" Obie said.

"She's bringing in her Pocahontas costume."

"Uh-oh," Obie said.

"She'll get the part, I know she will," Katie said. "She'll get to say, 'A bright and graceful child am I, about nine years of age . . .' " Katie sighed.

"Know what?" Obie said. "Pocahontas wasn't even at the first Thanksgiving."

"I know," Katie said. "But Mrs. Henry

32

said we could put her in the program anyway. 'Cause everyone wanted it. All the girls."

"Why don't you get a Pocahontas costume?" Obie said.

Katie sighed again. "Mom says I can't have anything more till Christmas," she said.

Obie was quiet for a minute. Then he said, "I know."

"What?" Katie said.

"We could make a costume!" Obie said. "My brown bathrobe. You can have it. It's itchy anyway. We'll just cut off the bottom so it's kind of raggedy."

"Like a Pocahontas dress!" Katie said. But then she thought of something. "Mom might get mad," she said.

"It's my bathrobe," Obie said.

"What about the hair?" Katie said. "I don't have black hair. Or even straight hair. Like Tiffany's."

"The Halloween box in the attic," Obie said. "You were a witch for Halloween. We could find the wig. Black, straight hair."

"Yeah!" Katie said. She began to smile. Obie had such good ideas. She'd been right to count on him.

But suddenly Obie was frowning.

"What?" Katie said.

"Maybe Mrs. Henry won't pick Tiffany. Or you," Obie said. "Maybe she'll pick Tawana."

"Tawana?" Katie said. "How come?"

"Because she has pretty black hair. Real hair," Obie said. He smiled and sighed. "It's long and straight, just like the real Pocahontas."

Katie thought about that. Tawana would be a perfect Pocahontas. She even looked like Pocahontas, with her smooth tan skin.

"She won't choose Tawana," she said. "Do you think?"

"She might," Obie said.

Katie frowned at her brother. "You're mean," she said.

Obie looked down. He picked at a scab. "Maybe she won't," he said. "Maybe she'll choose you. If you have a black wig and a brown Pocahontas dress."

"That's what I think," Katie said. And she crossed her fingers and hoped they were right.

The Grump

The next morning, Katie put her Pocahontas costume in her backpack. She had the brown bathrobe that she and Obie had cut so it was raggedy at the bottom. She had the black wig. And she had her old pink ballet slippers. The ballet slippers looked a little funny, but they were the closest she had to moccasins.

She left for school super-early. She was still on her best behavior and didn't want to miss the bus.

When she got on the bus, she thought about telling Amelia about her costume, but decided not to. Amelia might feel jealous. She couldn't wait to show the costume to Mrs. Henry, though.

But when they got to school, there was a surprise. No Mrs. Henry.

Instead, there was a substitute teacher standing in the front of the room. She was short and round, with a face like a pancake. Her teeth kind of stuck out. Her name was Mrs. Morris, and she was the meanest substitute in the whole world.

"Pick up your name tag from my desk, please," Mrs. Morris said to each person. "Stick it on so I know who you are."

Katie went up to Mrs. Henry's desk. She looked through the tags till she found her name. She felt a little worried in her stomach. She didn't like scary teachers. She looked over her shoulder at Mrs. Morris.

Mrs. Morris was trying to help Emil take off his boots. Emil's grandma always made him wear boots, even when it wasn't raining or snowing. Emil was leaning against the blackboard holding on, while Mrs. Morris stood in front of him, pulling at his foot.

"Mrs. Morris?" Katie said.

"In a minute, Missy," she said.

Very grumpy.

Suddenly Emil plopped to the floor as the boot shot off.

Mrs. Morris almost fell over backwards.

Katie tried hard not to laugh. She put a hand on her mouth.

She'd been going to tell Mrs. Morris that Mrs. Henry had Emil sit down on the floor in front of her to pull off the boots. The boots slid off easily that way and nobody fell down.

But it was too late to tell it now.

"Something funny, Missy?" Mrs. Morris said, looking at Katie.

Katie shook her head and looked at the floor. She went to her desk and slid into her seat. Everybody in class was very quiet.

"I don't like Mrs. Morris," Amelia whispered to Katie.

"I think I hate her," Katie said.

She pulled the backing off her name tag and stuck the tag on her sweater. She looked down at it. It was kind of crooked.

She peeled it off. Fuzzies from her pink sweater came off with it.

She picked at the fuzzies, but they were stuck to the gluey backing. She blew on them, but they stayed stuck. She sighed and put the tag back on.

It didn't stick so well anymore. The edges stuck out. Like Obie's ears, Katie thought.

She looked over at Tiffany. Tiffany had a big box on her desk.

Katie thought she knew what was inside — the Pocahontas stuff and the costume dolls.

Katie put her backpack on her desk.

"All right, boys and girls," Mrs. Morris said. "I'm your substitute teacher for today and probably for the next week, too."

Somebody made a groaning sound. Mrs. Morris said, "It won't be that bad." She smiled.

Right away, Katie felt a little better.

"What's wrong with Mrs. Henry?" Emil asked.

"Maybe chicken pox," Mrs. Morris said. She made a sad face.

Tiffany laughed out loud. "Chicken pox?" she said.

"Well, I don't think it's funny," Mrs. Morris said. "It can be serious when grown-ups get children's diseases."

Tiffany's face got red.

"What's your name?" Mrs. Morris said. She pointed a finger at Tiffany's name tag. "I can't read that."

"Tiffany," Tiffany said quietly.

Katie noticed that Tiffany's name tag was upside-down. Tiffany hadn't noticed, though.

Mrs. Morris wrote something down in the teacher book — maybe a bad mark next to Tiffany's name.

"Now, boys and girls," Mrs. Morris said, looking up from the teacher book. "Today we're going to finish plans for the breakfast. And maybe tomorrow we'll work on the program. Now let's begin with the morning exercises."

She didn't say, Let's stand for the pledge, so nobody moved.

Tiffany raised her hand.

"Yes, Tiffany?" Mrs. Morris said.

"I couldn't bring the dolls yet," Tiffany said. "But I have the Pocahontas costume. Do you want to see it?"

Mrs. Morris looked down at the teacher book again. She looked at it for a long time. Then she looked up at Tiffany. "Did Mrs. Henry say you're going to be Pocahontas?" she said, frowning.

"She said maybe," Tiffany said, nodding.

Katie turned and made a face at Tiffany. Mrs. Henry hadn't said maybe. She hadn't said anything!

"She told you that?" Mrs. Morris said.

"Sort of," Tiffany said. "I mean, I asked if I could be."

"I'm sure you did," Mrs. Morris said.

"I wouldn't count on it, though. Now, class, it's time for morning exercises."

She held out her hands, palms up, like she was checking for rain. She wiggled her fingers.

People looked at each other.

Katie said, "Mrs. Henry always says, Please stand for the pledge."

Mrs. Morris smiled. "Please stand for the pledge," she said. She said it nicely.

Everybody stood up.

Katie turned to the flag. But when she did, she noticed Tiffany. Her eyes were shiny and she was blinking hard. Her face was very red.

Katie inched closer to Tiffany. She patted her hand.

"Your name tag's upside-down," she whispered.

A Yucky
Mud Puddle

The rest of the morning was boring. A little scary, too. Katie wished and wished that Mrs. Henry would get better fast.

There were two good things that happened, though. First, Mrs. Morris handed out the list of each person's job for the Thanksgiving breakfast. Katie's job was to help churn the butter. That meant that she had to turn and turn and turn this big handle on a butter churn. Mrs. Henry was going to bring it in — an old-fashioned butter churn. It sounded like fun to Katie. She was glad she hadn't gotten the boring job of setting the tables like Amelia got. Katie did that at home.

The second good thing was that Tiffany didn't get to show off her Pocahontas costume. Mrs. Morris said she didn't even want to talk about the program until the breakfast plans were finished. She made Tiffany put her box in the coat closet.

Finally, though, the morning was almost over and it was time for recess. Outside, Katie ran for the swings. She was so glad to be away from Mrs. Morris. "Watch this!" she shouted to Amelia.

She jumped on the swing and pumped and pumped until she was up super-high. "Now watch out!" she yelled.

She jumped. She sailed out, then down. She landed in a yucky mud puddle.

"Oh, bluck!" she said.

Amelia came over to help her up. "You looked like a bird," she said.

"I feel like a pig," Katie said. She stared at her new pink sneakers. They were really muddy.

"Hey!" Amelia said. "Maybe there's frogs in this puddle!"

"We could bring one in and put it on Mrs. Morris's desk," Katie said. But she didn't really mean it.

Amelia bent to take a better look.

Katie bent, too.

No frogs.

She sighed and stood up. She looked at her feet. They looked disgusting. They felt disgusting, too.

"Maybe I should put on those ballet slippers," she said.

"What ballet slippers?" Amelia said.

Katie looked down at her feet. She rubbed one foot on the other. "I didn't mean ballet slippers," she said. "I meant something else."

"Oh," Amelia said.

"I meant my gym shoes," Katie said. Even though she knew her gym shoes were home.

"Hurry," Amelia said.

Katie crossed the school yard. Mrs.

Morris was standing by the door, her arms folded. She was watching Arthur and Bobby Bork. Bobby was being a Power Ranger, kicking out at something.

Arthur was zooming around him. It looked like Arthur was being a bird.

Mrs. Morris shook a finger at the boys. "Not too close!" she said. "Somebody will get hurt."

"Mrs. Morris," Katie said, "can I go change my shoes?"

Mrs. Morris looked at Katie's feet. "Uh-oh," she said.

"Mud," Katie said.

"You have dry shoes?" Mrs. Morris asked.

Katie nodded.

"Okay, then," she said. "Go on inside. And get a drink of water. You look hot."

Katie went into school. The hall was very quiet. She looked in all the rooms as she went down the hall.

In every classroom she passed, people

were reading and studying. In Mr. Grover's kindergarten room, a little kid was doing show and tell. He was wearing a Mickey Mouse shirt and striped pants. It looked like pajamas. He was holding a gerbil cupped in one hand.

Katie stopped to watch. She loved gerbils. Her class used to have two gerbils, Anthony and Jennifer. But one night they pushed the top off their cage and ran away. Nobody ever saw them again. Katie hoped they ran away to the cafeteria so they could get food.

Katie saw Mr. Grover watching her. He signaled with his finger for her to go on.

She hurried down the hall.

It was quiet in the classroom. She went to her desk in back. She opened up her backpack and pulled out her old pink ballet slippers. She wondered what Amelia would say.

She slid off her shoes and looked around. Where to put the muddy shoes? She couldn't put them in the backpack. They would mess up her Pocahontas costume.

Maybe in the coat closet? They could dry off in there.

She put on the ballet slippers and carried her shoes to the coat closet. Inside, on the floor, she could see Tiffany's box, in the cubby under her coat hook.

Katie looked all around her.

Nobody around.

Quietly, she bent over. She slid the box out and opened it.

Inside was an entire Pocahontas costume. There was a brown dress with a belt that looked like a rope. The dress was all pointy-like around the bottom, but it didn't look raggedy like Katie's bathrobe. There were little brown moccasins with beads on them, beautiful beads. There was a shiny necklace. And there was a beaded headband. The whole thing was beautiful, the most beautiful thing Katie had ever seen.

Tiffany was right — it was spectacular.

Katie sighed. And then she couldn't

help it. She lifted out the dress. She stood up and held it up to her and twirled around.

She was Pocahontas, dancing for the Indian chief. She was beautiful, and she had straight black hair.

She slid the headband over her hair. She tossed her head.

She danced some more.

She heard a noise. Feet sounds. Lots of feet sounds. Her class was coming back.

Quickly, she folded up the dress. She put it back in the box on top of the moccasins. Then she jammed the cover onto the box and shoved it back in the cubby.

She came out of the closet just as the kids were getting to the door.

She went straight to her desk, smoothing her hair.

And felt the headband.

She started back for the coat closet, but Mrs. Morris was already in the doorway.

Katie snatched off the headband. She crumpled it up in her hand. She looked all around, then stuffed the headband in her desk.

She felt very scared. Her face and ears were hot. She'd fix everything, though. Later she'd put the headband back. She would.

7

The New Girl

The next day was Friday. Obie still had chicken pox. Mrs. Henry still had chicken pox. And Katie wished like anything that she had chicken pox.

She wanted to be anywhere but in school.

Tiffany was at her desk, pulling everything out. Her leaf collection pasted on red paper. A book called *City Arithmetic*.

"It's not here, Mrs. Morris!" she said. "I told you so."

"Don't be fresh," Mrs. Morris said. But she didn't sound too mad.

"Somebody stole it!" Tiffany said.

"Now why would anyone do that?" Mrs. Morris said. "Now, class, I want everyone to take everything out of their desks and see if you can find Tiffany's headband. Maybe somebody picked it up by accident."

Katie could feel her heart pounding hard.

It had been an accident. But how could she give the headband back now?

"It's a good opportunity to clean out your desks, anyway," Mrs. Morris said. "Who wants to go up and down the aisles with the wastebasket?"

"I do!" Arthur said.

"I'm the wastebasket person this week!" Tawana said.

"Then go on, Tawana," Mrs. Morris said.

Tawana started up and down the aisles.

People were pulling stuff out of their desks — crumpled-up papers and broken bits of pencils and even old food and shoes.

Bobby Bork always had food in his desk.

Mrs. Henry was always making him clean it out. She said it attracted mice.

Katie didn't know why that was bad. Obie once had pet mice. They were fun. The gerbils were lost, so maybe the mice could become their class pets.

Next to Katie, Amelia took out a bunch of stuff and put it on her desk for the trash. There were about a zillion broken pencils that looked like a dog had chewed them. There were some broken barrettes. And there were snarled-up rubber hairbands.

"Look!" Amelia said to Katie. She held up one of the hairbands. It still had hair twisted up it in. "My hair," she said. "Gross."

Katie nodded. But she couldn't answer. Her heart was pounding too hard, and she could feel tears coming up in her eyes.

She couldn't pull stuff out of her desk. What if the headband came out by mistake?

She bent over so that her head was almost inside her desk.

Black inside. She couldn't see a thing.

She stuck her hand in.

Way at the back, she could feel the headband.

Mrs. Morris was standing next to her. "Come on, Missy!" she said. "I know you have plenty of trash in there."

Katie swallowed hard. "I'm doing it," she said.

"Let's see," Mrs. Morris said.

Carefully, Katie let go of the headband. She reached for stuff from the front of her desk.

Her spelling book. Her pencil box. The little sharpener shaped like a unicorn.

She laid them carefully on her desk.

Mrs. Morris nodded at her. "Good! Keep it up," she said. "I know there's more in there." She moved away down the aisle.

Tiffany leaned over Katie's desk. "I know you stole it," she said. "You're a thief!"

"Am not!" Katie said.

She made a mad face at Tiffany. But she could feel her ears get hot.

She wasn't a thief. She didn't steal. She

had made a big mistake, though.

She bent over her desk again.

She stuck her hand way in the back.

She could feel the headband there still.

Maybe she could just scrunch it up in a ball in her fist? Then she could take it out and slide it into her pocket. Then, somehow, she could get it back in the box in the coat closet.

Or would Tiffany notice?

She looked over at Tiffany.

Tiffany was watching her, her eyes squinched up.

Just then the classroom door opened. It was Mr. Collins, the principal, and he had a new kid with him.

It was a girl, a really tall girl with the blackest hair Katie had ever seen. It hung straight down and was tucked behind her ears. Like Pocahontas. She had bangs that almost came to her eyes.

She had a beautiful red headband holding the hair back.

Katie sighed and felt her own hair.

Not long. Not black. Not like Poca-hontas.

"Here's a new student for you, Mrs. Morris," Mr. Collins said. "This is Maria and she's come all the way from Puerto Rico."

"*¡Buenos días!*" Tiffany said, very loud.

Mr. Collins turned and smiled at Tiffany.

"How lovely!" he said. He turned to Maria. "What do you say, Maria?" he said.

Maria was staring at her feet. "Hi," she muttered.

Tiffany kept smiling at Maria, like she was waiting to have a conversation in Spanish or something.

Katie quickly reached inside her desk.

She grabbed the headband and crumpled it inside her fist.

She looked over at Tiffany.

Tiffany was still looking at the new kid.

Katie slid the headband out of her desk. Then she bent over and stuffed it into her backpack. She stuffed it way down deep.

She took a deep breath. She sat up straight and tall.

"Where should Maria sit?" Mr. Collins said to Mrs. Morris.

"Here!" Tiffany called out.

She pointed to an empty chair. It was behind Katie, and practically right next to Tiffany.

Margaret Anne used to sit there before she moved to San Diego last month.

Mr. Collins looked at Mrs. Morris. "Is that all right with you?" he said.

Mrs. Morris nodded. "Fine," she said. "If Mrs. Henry wants to change it when she gets back, she can."

Maria came down the aisle.

Katie looked up and smiled at her.

Maria didn't smile back. She was frowning hard.

Katie didn't care.

She had the headband and it was hidden. Nobody would look in her backpack. Somehow she'd get it back to Tiffany.

But then she had a new bad thought.

Mrs. Henry was always extra-nice to new kids. And Maria looked even more like Pocahontas than Tawana did.

Katie sighed. Maybe it would be better if Mrs. Henry didn't come back too soon.

8

Obie's Good Idea

All that day and over the weekend, Katie worried. She had the headband out of her desk now. But she hadn't had a single chance on Friday to get into the coat closet alone. How could she put it back?

Then, by Monday morning, she had an idea. Maybe she didn't have to put it back! She could just throw it away, that's what. She could stick it in the trash pail out back. Or she could flush it down the toilet or the disposal. Nobody would know.

Nobody would know that she had

stolen something, that she was a thief. Just like Tiffany said.

Except that then Tiffany wouldn't have her headband. Her wonderful beaded headband. It would be gone for good.

Katie sighed and worried some more.

There was one good thing that happened, though. Obie was better. He hadn't broken out in any new spots in three days, and all the old spots were healing over. He could go back to school. He did look pretty scabby, though.

While they walked to the bus that morning, Katie swung her backpack around in front of her. "Obie?" she said. "What's the baddest thing you ever did?"

"Stuck an eraser in my ear," Obie said.

Katie stopped swinging her backpack. She looked at Obie. "You did?" she said. "I don't remember."

"Yes, you do," Obie said. "Remember that time I took the eraser off the end of my pencil and I stuck it in my ear? I just wanted to see if it would fit, but then I couldn't get it out again."

"Oh, I remember," Katie said. "You wouldn't tell Mom."

Obie nodded. "Except after a couple days it hurt. And I couldn't hear too well. I got scared."

Katie nodded. She was remembering it all now. "Then you told Mom and Dad, and they took you to the doctor. And then you had to go to the hospital so they could take it out."

"Yeah," Obie said. "I was scared."

"But that wasn't really bad, was it?" Katie said. "I mean, it was just a mistake. You didn't . . . steal anything or anything, right?"

"No-oo," Obie said. "It was my own eraser."

They had gotten to the bus stop, and they both sat down on the curb. Nobody was there yet, but Katie knew it wasn't because they had missed the bus. It was because they were early. With Obie, they were always early.

"Obie?" Katie said. "What if you did steal something?"

"I wouldn't," Obie said.

"But what if you did? By accident?" Katie said.

Obie shrugged. "If it's by accident, it's not stealing."

"Oh," Katie said.

"But you'd still have to give it back," Obie said.

"Yeah," Katie said. She looked over at him. He was poking the toe of his sneaker into the muddy leaves that lay along the edge of the curb. She knew he was looking for worms. She and Obie were always looking for worms.

"Once," he said, "I came home from baseball practice and had a baseball in my bag by accident. I brought it back next time."

Katie picked up a stick and started poking in the leaves, looking, too. "Did anybody

see you bring it back?" she said.

He shrugged. "I just gave it to the coach."

"Oh," Katie said. She poked some more, carefully though, so she wouldn't hurt the worms.

There weren't any worms, though. Just mud.

She stood up and wiped her hands on her jacket. "Too cold for worms," she told Obie.

"They're hibernating," Obie said. He stood up, too, and wiped his muddy foot on his jeans. "Another time," he said, "I took the playground ball home."

"By accident, too?" Katie said.

Obie frowned and rubbed at his sneakers some more. "Sort of," he said.

"What happened?" Katie asked.

Obie looked up. Arthur was running toward the bus stop. Bobby Bork was running with him. They were kicking out at each other, pretending to be Power Rangers.

"Obie?" Katie said.

Obie waved at his friends. "I just left it on the playground next day," he said. "Like it was there all along."

"And then what?" Katie said.

Obie started running toward his friends. He put up his hands like he was morphing into a Ranger, too.

"And then what?" Katie called to him.

"Then the school people found it," Obie yelled back.

He and Bobby and Arthur began circling each other.

Katie sat down on the curb again. She was smiling.

She reached into her backpack and felt for the headband.

She'd thought of leaving it home, but was glad she'd decided not to. She took it out now and stuffed it in the pocket of her jacket. She'd drop it on the playground. Then Tiffany would come out at recess and she'd find it there. She'd think she'd dropped it by accident.

Katie smiled. She thought about Tiffany finding the headband and being so happy. She thought about Mrs. Morris and how happy she'd be. Katie felt happy, too. She thought maybe she even liked Tiffany and Mrs. Morris a little bit.

She smiled again. She was lucky Obie was her twin. He always had such good ideas.

 **9**

Mrs. Henry
Is Back!

At school, when the bell rang to line up, Katie was the slowest to get in line, the very slowest. She was even slower than Bobby Bork.

She waited till everyone had lined up. Then she took teensy-weensy steps across the school yard. She ended up at the very end of the line. Everybody was facing straight ahead.

Katie held tight to the headband in her pocket. She could feel her heart beating thumpy-hard in her chest.

After a minute, the second bell rang. The line moved.

All but Katie.

She let the whole line get far ahead. She looked all around.

Nobody was watching her.

She took a deep breath. She pulled out the headband. She let go of it. It dropped alongside the fence.

Done! She smiled. Already, she was feeling better. The headband would be found and nobody would know who had dropped it there.

She looked down at it. It lay there in the dirt by the fence, the little beads twinkling in the sun. For a minute, she felt worried about it, laying in the dirt. But it would be found soon.

She turned back and hurried to join the line. She hadn't felt this happy since before Mrs. Henry got sick.

When they got into school, there was something else to feel extra-happy about: Mrs. Henry was back!

No more stinky Mrs. Morris.

"But you had chicken pox!" Katie said to Mrs. Henry when they were all seated. "I thought you'd be sick a long time."

Mrs. Henry smiled at the class. "I thought so, too," she said. "But the doctor said it was probably just a virus. Sometimes you get spots with that, too."

"Mrs. Henry!" Tiffany called out. "Now will you tell us about the program? Mrs. Morris never did. Do you want to see my Pocahontas costume?" She jumped up. "I'll get it!"

Katie quickly bent to her backpack and put it on her desk. Her costume was still in it.

"Not just yet, Tiffany," Mrs. Henry said, holding up a hand. She smiled. "Sit down now. I promise we'll talk about the program tomorrow. Promise. Today, I need to catch up with what's been happening here since I've been gone. Are we ready for morning exercises? Let's stand for the pledge."

Everybody stood up.

"Mrs. Morris forgot to tell us to stand up," Katie said. "I had to remind her."

Mrs. Henry smiled at Katie and put a finger on her lips.

They all turned to the flag. They said the pledge and then sang "My Country 'Tis of Thee," Katie's favorite of all the morning songs.

After they sat back down, Mrs. Henry said, "I hear we have a new student." She smiled at Maria. "Welcome, Maria," she said. "Is that a good seat back there?"

Katie turned to look at Maria sitting behind her. Maria was frowning at her fingernails.

Katie noticed that Maria frowned a lot. She also didn't talk much. But she had sparkle fingernail polish.

Katie looked at her own nails. Naked. Her mom said no polish till she was ten. At least. She sighed.

"It's okay here," Maria said.

"We want you to be happy, Maria," Mrs. Henry said.

74

She waited, but Maria didn't say anything more. She just started picking at her sparkle nail polish.

Katie wondered if Maria was sad. Or lonely.

Katie thought she would hate to move and go to a new school.

"All right, boys and girls," Mrs. Henry said. "Why don't you tell me what happened while I was gone? Raise your hands if you have something special to tell me. Do you know that I missed you?"

Katie turned back and smiled at Mrs. Henry. She was glad Mrs. Henry was back. She hated scary teachers like Mrs. Morris. She wondered why people got to be teachers if they didn't like kids.

Mrs. Henry liked kids. Katie thought maybe she'd be a teacher when she got big.

"I know something that happened," Emil said. He forgot to raise his hand.

"Tell me," Mrs. Henry said. "And raise your hand next time."

"Mrs. Morris doesn't take off boots

very good," Emil said. "Not like you. I fell down."

Amelia raised her hand. "And Mrs. Morris almost fell down, too," she said.

Mrs. Henry looked surprised. "Didn't anyone tell her how to do it?"

"I tried to," Katie said. "But Mrs. Morris just said, 'In a minute, Missy!'" Katie made her voice grumpy like Mrs. Morris's.

"Oh," Mrs. Henry said.

She looked like she was trying not to smile.

Tiffany raised her hand. "Something bad happened when you were gone," she said.

"Oh?" Mrs. Henry said. "I'm sorry. What was it?"

Katie suddenly felt her heart thumping hard again.

"Somebody stole my headband," Tiffany said. "My Pocahontas headband!"

"They didn't STEAL it!" Katie burst out.

She glared at Tiffany. She could feel her face get hot.

"No!" Mrs. Henry said. "Nobody would steal it. It must have gotten misplaced."

Tiffany shook her head hard. Her long, straight hair swung from side to side.

"We looked," she said. "We even cleaned out our desks."

Mrs. Henry looked troubled. "Are you sure you didn't just misplace it?" she said.

Again Tiffany swung her hair. Hard.

"We looked everywhere," she said.

"Did not," Katie said. "Just in the classroom."

"Well, where else could it be, Katie?" Mrs. Henry said.

Katie looked at Mrs. Henry. She thought of saying, On the playground. But she was afraid. Maybe Mrs. Henry would think she was a thief. Mrs. Henry wouldn't like her anymore. She just lifted her shoulders up to her ears.

"Maybe on the school bus!" Obie said. He had forgotten to raise his hand, so he raised it while he was talking. "Or in the cafeteria or library," he said. "Or maybe even outside. Maybe she dropped it somewhere."

"Did you look in all those places?" Mrs. Henry asked Tiffany. "How about in the office in Lost and Found?"

Tiffany shook her head. "It's not there," she said.

"Did you look?" Mrs. Henry asked.

Tiffany shook her head no.

"Well, let's look today," Mrs. Henry said. "We'll look everywhere we go today, playground, library. It will turn up."

Katie took a deep breath.

It would turn up. It would all be better now. Now all she had to worry about was the program. And getting to be Pocahontas. But even that didn't worry her too much. For now, she felt a whole lot better inside.

10

The Search

Everywhere they went that day, they looked for the headband. In the library, before they had story time, they asked Mrs. Rubin, the librarian, to check her Lost and Found. While she looked there, the kids looked around under the tables and by the little kids' toys and everywhere.

Katie pretended to be looking hard like everyone else.

They did the same thing during music time. They looked in the instrument closet and under the bandstand and everything.

No headband.

Finally it was recess time, playground time.

"Don't forget to look for the head-band!" Mrs. Henry reminded everyone on their way out.

Katie nodded and raced outside with Amelia.

She wondered if she should go straight to the fence and find the headband, but thought that Tiffany would be too suspicious. She decided she'd slowly make her way over to the fence with Amelia. Maybe Amelia could find it.

But when they looked along the fence, Katie didn't see it. No headband. Nothing but dead leaves.

Katie put her fists on her hips. She looked all around. It had to be there!

She and Amelia both kicked their feet into the leaves. Katie kicked hard, sending the leaves flying into the air. The leaves made a nice swishy sound. But there wasn't any headband under them.

"Not here," Amelia said. "Let's swing."

"In a minute," Katie said.

"Hurry!" Amelia said, and she ran for the swings.

Katie bent over. She dug through the leaves with her hands. She turned over bunches and bunches of leaves. Nothing. Nothing but more leaves. She dug some more. She found a frozen mitten. She found a wheel off a toy car. She found half a tennis ball. But she didn't find the headband. She could feel this funny feeling come inside her, like she was sick.

How could it be gone? Where could it go? It had to be there. She'd *put* it there.

The funny feeling got worse.

She'd lost the headband. It was gone. The beautiful, beautiful headband. The Pocahontas headband.

She bent down and looked again. She looked for a really long time. She could feel tears come into her eyes. The headband was gone and it was all her fault.

"Katie!" Amelia yelled. "Look at me. I'm a bird."

Katie looked.

Amelia was zooming around the playground, her arms out.

Tawana was perched on top of the climbing bars. "Me, too!" she yelled. "I'm in my nest."

"I'm the mama bird!" Tiffany said. She ran toward the climbing bars. "I'm in charge of the nest," she yelled.

Katie ran over to join them. "You have to go get worms," she told Tiffany. She blocked Tiffany's way onto the bars. "Go! That's what mama birds do."

"Unh-uh," Tiffany said. "My baby's already been fed."

Katie looked up at Tawana. "You have not, have you?" she called.

"Peep-peep, I'm hungry!" Tawana said.

Her voice sounded little and hungry, like a real bird's.

"See?" Katie said. "She's hungry."

"I'm not doing it," Tiffany said.

"It's the rules," Katie said. "Go!"

She gave Tiffany a little push. But just a little one.

Tiffany stepped backwards. She bumped into Bobby Bork.

Bobby gave her a little push, too.

Tiffany went down. Right on her knees.

Bobby ran off.

"You pushed!" Tiffany said to Katie.

"Only sort of," Katie said. "It was Bobby, too."

She reached to help Tiffany up.

Tiffany pushed her away and stood up.

"Uh-oh," Katie said.

Tiffany looked down.

Blood. And a hole in her tights.

"My best tights!" Tiffany said. She looked like she was going to cry.

Mrs. Henry came over. She put an arm around Tiffany. "Poor thing," she said. "You can go in to the nurse. But it doesn't look too bad."

"Katie did it!" Tiffany said. "Katie pushed me."

"Only a little," Katie said.

Mrs. Henry got a frowny look on her face. "I'm surprised at you, Katie," she said. "Go with Tiffany to the nurse. You can help her."

Katie made her breath come out loud. But she didn't answer back.

She just walked with Tiffany to the school.

Tiffany pretended to be limping. She bent over and held onto her knee.

They got to the school door. Tiffany waited while Katie opened it and held it for her.

It was quiet in the halls.

They went down to the nurse's office. Mrs. Holt was the nurse. She was the nicest person in the whole school, next to Mrs. Henry. She had Band-Aids and drinks of water and lollipops if you got really hurt.

But she wasn't in her office. There was a big sign on the door. It said: BACK IN A MINUTE. PLEASE WAIT.

Whenever the sign said that, it meant you had to sit and wait on the bench outside the door.

Tiffany sat down on the bench. She bent over her knee, holding it.

Katie sat down, too. She left a big space between her and Tiffany.

Tiffany made little hurting sounds.

"It doesn't hurt that much," Katie said.

Tiffany looked over at her. Her eyes were wet and shiny. She blinked and looked away.

Crybaby, Katie thought. But she felt her own eyes get wet.

She hadn't really meant to hurt Tiffany. She hadn't meant to lose her headband, either.

Mrs. Holt came down the hall, her office key in her hand. She looked at Katie and Tiffany. "Two sick chickies?" she asked, smiling.

"No. Just me!" Tiffany said. "My knee!" She made it sound really pitiful, and she held out her leg.

"I'm helping her!" Katie said. She said it fast and loud, so Tiffany wouldn't get to say about it being Katie's fault.

Mrs. Holt smiled at Katie. "Good for you," she said. "Like a real nurse."

Katie looked down at the floor.

Mrs. Holt put an arm around Tiffany. She helped her up. They started into the office. Tiffany was limping even harder.

"We'll fix this in no time," Mrs. Holt said. "We'll just wash it up and give you a Band-Aid. I bet we can even find a lollipop for you."

She turned back to Katie. "Thank you for bringing her," she said.

Katie nodded, but she didn't move.

"You can go back to your room now," Mrs. Holt said.

Katie stood up and started down the hall.

She sighed. She thought Mrs. Holt should have offered her a lollipop, too. Or at least a Band-Aid.

11

I Hate Meat Loaf

That night at supper, Sam and Matt were arguing. Sam said Matt lost their soccer ball. Matt said Sam left it at the field. Baby-Child was hammering on his high chair tray with his spoon, yelling his newest word — *Quack!* — over and over again. Obie was trying to tell Mom about the Thanksgiving breakfast and his job of squashing up cranberries. Mom was trying to hush Baby-Child, and Dad was trying to shush Sam and Matt. Only Katie was very, very quiet.

All she could think about was the headband. It was gone. And it was all her fault.

She had felt sick all day in school about it, really, really sick. She even had a pain, right in her middle.

And now she had a new worry — not only did Tawana look like Pocahontas, but the new girl, Maria, did too. And Mrs. Henry was being extra-nice to Maria.

Katie pushed her meat loaf around her plate. She wished she could make the meat loaf disappear, just like the headband had disappeared. She hated meat loaf. She had even left a note on Mom's desk when she got home and found out about the meat loaf. She wrote it with her favorite, brightest, red marker. The note said:

I hate meat loaf.
Meat loaf is gross and disgusting.
Meat loaf is worse than eating worms.
I will not eat meat loaf tonight.

But when Mom read it, she just smiled and said, "You're eating it, Katie. And that's that."

But that wasn't that.

Katie wasn't going to eat it.

She broke it up into little pieces. She pushed the pieces around her plate. She made a line of meat loaf pieces on one side of her plate.

She made another line on the other side.

She put her mashed potatoes in the middle. She slid some bites of meat loaf under her mashed potatoes.

My fault, my fault, my fault, she thought.

"Eat up, Katie," Daddy said.

"I'm eating," Katie said.

She rolled some peas around her plate. Peas were almost as bad as meat loaf.

"It doesn't look to me like you're eating," Daddy said.

Katie made a face. She put down her fork and sighed. "I don't feel good," she said.

"What's wrong?" Daddy said.

Katie sighed again. "Chicken pox," she said. "Probably."

"Chicken pox, really?" Daddy said. He sounded worried.

"Really," Katie said. She made her face look really sad.

Maybe she would get chicken pox. Then she wouldn't have to go back to school. Maybe she'd get so sick she wouldn't ever have to go back. Maybe she'd end up in a hospital like that kid on television who had school from his hospital bed. Tiffany would be so jealous. And she'd probably forget all about her stupid headband. Maybe she'd even buy a headband and give it to Katie to make her feel happier for having to spend the rest of her life in a hospital.

"Does she have a fever?" Daddy said to Mom. "Spots?"

Mom shook her head. "It's just meat loaf," she said.

"It's what?" Daddy said.

"Meat loaf," Mom said. "That's all."

"Oh," Daddy said.

"And I even left out the onions," Mom said.

"It's not meat loaf!" Katie said. She could feel tears welling up in her eyes. "I'm sick!"

"Sick where?" Daddy said.

Katie stared down at her plate.

Her brothers had gotten very quiet. Even Baby-Child wasn't banging at his tray anymore.

"Tell me, Katie," Daddy said. "What hurts?"

"Here," Katie said. She put a hand on her chest, right in the middle. "I think it's . . ." But she couldn't think what could make you feel so bad in your chest like that. Except for the stolen headband. That's right where she could feel it.

"A heart attack, I bet," Obie said. "I saw it on TV."

Sam and Matt both burst out laughing.

"Little kids don't get heart attacks," Sam said.

"I'm not that little!" Katie said. She glared at Sam.

Sometimes she hated him. Matt, too. Even Baby-Child.

Suddenly she burst into tears.

She jumped up from the table. She ran up the stairs to her room and slammed the door.

Then she opened it up and slammed it again. And then she did it again.

She plopped down on her bed.

They were all mean. Even Mom. And Dad. It wasn't meat loaf. It was the headband. And she couldn't tell anybody.

She thought of calling Grandpa. He was her best friend, practically. But then she didn't think she could tell him, either. Well, maybe. But he couldn't make it any better either, unless he could come and find the headband. And nobody could do that.

She lay back on her bed and hugged her bear.

She sighed. She turned over and picked up her red marker that was still where she'd left it on the bed. She rolled it around in her fingers.

Suddenly she had an idea. She sat up. She took the top off the marker pen. She pulled up her shirt. She made a dot on her stomach. She made another dot. And then another.

She got up and went over to the mirror. She poked her stomach out toward the mirror.

Did it look like Obie's stomach, like a connect-a-dot picture?

She didn't think so.

She dotted on a few more dots.

She pulled back and looked in the mirror. Better. Not too many spots and not too few spots. Just enough. She remembered from Obie that you didn't get that many spots to begin with.

There was a knock on her door.

"What?" she said.

"Can I come in?" It was Daddy.

Katie pulled down her shirt. But then she had a new thought. She leaned forward to the mirror. She dotted a few dots on her cheeks.

"Katie?" Daddy called.

Katie went over to the bed and sat down. She stuck the marker under her bear. "Okay," she said. "You can come in."

Daddy came in and sat beside her. He took her hand.

"What's up, Toots?" he said, using his favorite pet name for her.

Katie shrugged. "Nothing."

"Don't want to tell me about it?" he said.

"I already did," Katie said. "I'm sick."

She turned to face him so he could see the spots. But he didn't seem to notice.

All he said was, "Oh." He nodded. "I see."

But he didn't. Katie knew that. She pulled her hand out of his.

She turned away and sighed. She picked at the bedspread. "Daddy?" she said softly. "Do little kids go to jail?"

 **12**

Really Sick

The next morning, Mom took Katie's temperature. She frowned over the thermometer as she took it out of Katie's mouth. But then she smiled and looked up at Katie. "Normal!" she said.

"It can't be normal!" Katie said. "Feel my forehead."

She had been holding her breath, making herself get hot. She knew she must have a fever by now.

Mom put a hand on Katie's forehead. She smiled again. "Cool as a cucumber," she

said. "Go up and get dressed. You're going to school and that's that."

Katie made a big frown at her mom but didn't say anything more. When Mom said "That's that!" it meant no argument, just like last night with the meat loaf.

Katie just made another big frown at Mom and went upstairs.

But she thought, Well, ha to you! I didn't eat meat loaf last night, so there.

But it didn't make her feel better.

Nothing could make her feel better. She'd lost the headband. Somebody in the bigger grades must have picked it up on their recess. Or maybe the janitor or somebody had found it. But there was no way Katie could ask about it and get it back.

She was a thief, just like Tiffany said. And her stomach did hurt and her head, too, no matter what Mom said. And no matter if she didn't have a fever. Also, her stomach was beginning to itch. She wondered if the colored marker made you itchy.

All the way to school, Katie worried

and felt sick. But at school, Mrs. Henry was finally handing out parts for the Thanksgiving program. Katie wondered if that would make her feel better. It would if she got the Pocahontas part.

They had finished all the morning exercises.

Mrs. Henry went up and down the aisles, handing each person a paper.

"Read what I give you, boys and girls," Mrs. Henry said. "This is each person's part. We'll rehearse later. I'll show you how it all fits together."

Katie looked over at Tiffany.

Tiffany had her eyes closed and her hands folded. She was saying something silently. Her lips were moving like she was saying a prayer.

Katie could read Tiffany's lips. She was saying, " 'A bright and graceful child am I' . . . oh please, oh please, oh please."

Katie thought of saying a prayer, too. "Oh please, oh please, oh please," she whispered, over and over.

Mrs. Henry got to Katie's desk. Katie took the paper.

She quickly read it.

It said:

"The people worked and built a ship, the *Mayflower*, to take them on a trip across the Atlantic."

Katie could feel water coming to her eyes. She blinked hard and stared down at her desk. Mrs. Henry was mean!

After a minute, Katie peeked over at Tiffany's desk, but she couldn't see her paper.

She bent over, pretending to be looking for something on the floor. She stretched her neck far out toward Tiffany.

Tiffany quickly put a hand over her paper.

Katie noticed that Tiffany's face was red and her eyes were super-shiny.

So Tiffany wasn't Pocahontas, either.

Katie couldn't help feeling a little happy about that.

She turned around to peek at Maria's

paper. Katie was good at reading upside-down. But she couldn't read the paper because Maria's fingers were spread out on top of it. She was coloring her fingernails with a red marker pen right over the sparkle polish.

Katie thought about doing that. Maybe that way she could have nail polish. Mom couldn't complain about that.

Katie turned to her friend Amelia.

Amelia made a sad face, and stuck out her paper for Katie to read.

Katie read: "In Plymouth time there were wild turkeys in the woods and meat to eat."

Katie made a sad face back, and showed her her paper. Then she turned and looked all around the room. She looked at Tawana. Tawana was frowning, a big, deep frown. It didn't look like Tawana was Pocahontas, either.

Katie sighed and leaned back in her seat. She put a hand on her stomach. She really felt very yucky, there in her stomach, and in her head, too.

"I don't understand my part, Mrs. Henry," Emil said.

He had forgotten to raise his hand again.

He was always forgetting.

Mrs. Henry just looked at him, her eyebrows up.

He clamped a hand on his mouth and raised his hand.

"Yes, Emil?" Mrs. Henry said, in her nicest voice.

"I don't understand this," Emil said. "It says, 'The wee bird flies above its nest.' What kind of bird is a wee bird?"

Mrs. Henry smiled. "It means a small bird, Emil," she said.

"Oh," Emil said.

Everybody started calling out at once then, asking about their parts.

But Obie was the only one with his hand up, so Mrs. Henry called on him.

"Yes, Obie?" she said. She put up a hand to shush the others.

"Mine has a birdling," Obie said. "What's a birdling?"

"What do you think?" Mrs. Henry said.

"A little bird?" Obie said.

"A wee one!" Emil said.

"That's right," Mrs. Henry said, smiling. "You're both right."

Mrs. Henry looked all around the room. Then she said, "Uh-oh."

Everybody got very quiet.

"I think I see some sad faces," Mrs. Henry said. "Why?"

Nobody said anything. Katie didn't know about the other girls, but she knew what was making her face sad.

"Nobody?" Mrs. Henry said. "Nobody's going to tell me?"

Tiffany put up her hand. "Who's going to be Pocahontas?" she said, really mad-like. "I have the whole costume and all. I told you that."

"I know, Tiffany," Mrs. Henry said,

kindly. "But I thought perhaps we should share."

"I'm not sharing my costume!" Tiffany said.

Mrs. Henry smiled and shook her head. "I didn't mean that," she said. "I meant we have a new girl and it might be nice to let her . . ."

That's when Katie spoke up. She didn't even raise her hand.

"Mrs. Henry," she said, "I think I'm going to be sick."

And she was.

Right on the middle of her desk.

13

Sort of Itchy

After that, Katie got to go home. Mom came and picked her up and took her home and tucked her into bed.

By the time Obie got home from school, Katie was covered with spots. Not red marker spots. Real ones. Chicken pox ones.

Obie came in and sat on her bed.

"Poor Katie," he said. "Do you itch?"

Katie lay back on her pillows. "Sort of," she said. "My back does. And my head hurts."

"Mine did, too," Obie said. "But it gets better soon."

"Obie," Katie said, "who got to be Pocahontas? Maria?"

Obie nodded. "But guess what?"

"What?" Katie said. She turned and wriggled her back against the pillow.

"Mrs. Henry said Tiffany could wear her Pocahontas costume, too, if she wanted," Obie said.

"They're both going to be Pocahontas?" Katie said.

Obie shook his head. "No. But Mrs. Henry said there were lots of Indian girls at the early Thanksgivings, so it would be okay."

"Oh," Katie said.

"Maybe you'll be better by then," Obie said. "You can wear yours, too."

Katie nodded but she didn't say anything.

After seeing Tiffany's costume, she didn't think much of hers. But she didn't want Obie to feel bad, since he'd given her his bathrobe.

"Know what, though?" Obie said. "Tiffany cried all day."

"Because she couldn't be Pocahontas?" Katie said.

Obie shrugged. "I guess. But she said it was because of the headband."

Katie picked at the blankets.

"Tiffany's a crybaby," Obie said.

"Yeah," Katie said. But she wondered if she'd cry, too, if she'd lost her beaded headband.

Obie went downstairs and Katie tried to lie still, not itching or anything.

But she couldn't get comfortable. She turned this way and that way. She pulled her pillow off her bed and threw it on the floor.

She sat back against the headboard.

Her back hurt, so she picked up the pillow again and tucked it behind her again.

Mom came in with some soup and crackers and juice.

But Katie just made a face at them,

and Mom left them on her bedside table and went back downstairs.

Katie picked up her tape player and put in her Sleeping Beauty tape. But the noise hurt her head and she turned it off.

She could hear her brothers playing downstairs. She could hear Baby-Child saying, "Quack, quack!" And she could hear Obie laughing. Baby-Child started squealing, like Obie was tickling him.

Katie sighed. She hated being sick. And itchy. And alone up here.

Suddenly she had a thought. She could talk to her grandparents. She could talk to Grandma and Great-Grandma, or the other ones, Grandpa and Grandma.

Or all of them. They always made her feel better. Grandpa especially.

She got up to go to Mom's room. She knew all their numbers by heart.

She started with Grandma and Great-Grandma. They lived together. But their phone just rang and rang. It didn't even have an answering machine.

Katie hung up and dialed her other grandma and grandpa.

This time it was answered right away. Grandpa.

"Hi, Grandpa," Katie said. "It's me."

"Katie!" Grandpa said. "How are you, my dear?"

Katie sighed. "Sick," she said. "I'm sick."

"Oh, I'm sorry!" Grandpa said. "What's wrong?"

"Chicken pox!" she said. "Yucky, blucky chicken pox."

"Oh my," Grandpa said. "Poor honey. Are you all itchy?"

Katie nodded. But then she remembered that people couldn't see her on the phone. She sometimes still forgot that. "Sort of itchy," she said.

"I'm sorry, sweetie," Grandpa said. "Are you stuck in bed?"

Again Katie nodded. Again she remembered. "Yes," she said. Then she added. "Grandpa, will you come visit?"

"I sure will," Grandpa said. "Grandma and I are coming for Thanksgiving. For Turkey Day!"

"Oh," Katie said.

"Just about ten days from now," Grandpa said.

"Oh," Katie said again.

Grandpa was quiet a minute. Then he said, "Does it seem like a long time away?"

Katie nodded. "Uh-huh," she said. "A really long time. Anyway, I hate Turkey Day."

"You do?" Grandpa said.

"All it is is trouble," Katie said. "In school, anyway."

"Tell you what," Grandpa said. "Maybe I can make a quick trip tomorrow just for the day. Would you like that?"

Katie smiled. "Yes!" she said.

"I won't get there till late, though, you know," Grandpa said. "It's a long trip."

"I know," Katie said. "But you'll come, right?"

"I'll come," Grandpa said.

"Oh, good," Katie said. "I'm glad."

"Now let me talk to your mom for a minute," Grandpa said.

"Okay," Katie said. She dropped the phone on the bed, then went to the top of the stairs.

"Mom!" she yelled. "Grandpa's on the phone. He wants to talk to you."

She heard her mom pick up the phone in the kitchen. Then she went and hung up the one in Mom's room.

She went back to her room and got into bed.

She was really very sleepy. And her head still hurt and she was still itchy. But she felt a whole lot better than she had just a minute before. Grandpa always made her feel better.

Always.

14

Quack, Quack

The next morning, Katie opened her eyes to see sunlight falling across her bed. The whole house was very quiet. She looked at the clock on her bedside table. Ten o'clock. That meant her brothers had already gone to school.

She sat up and pushed back the covers. She pulled up her pajama shirt. She looked at her stomach.

"Oh, yuck!" she said.

She started to scratch at an itchy place by her belly button, but then she stopped.

Mom said don't scratch. You'd get scars.

And you'd look like a monster, Sam had said.

Katie got up and went over to the mirror and looked.

Spotty. Like a fire dog.

"Oh, yuck!" she said again, very loud.

She went down the hall to the bathroom. When she came out, Mom was in the hallway, holding a small tray in one hand. She had Baby-Child tucked squirming under her other arm.

"Feel like breakfast?" Mom said.

"I feel spotty," Katie said.

"Get into bed," Mom said. "Eat a little and then we'll give you a nice bath."

"I don't want a nice bath," Katie said. "I want to be better."

But she got into bed and Mom put the tray down on her lap.

Baby-Child was already down on the floor. "Quack!" he said, his newest favorite word.

"Quack yourself," Mom said to him.

She closed the door so he couldn't creep out, and then came and sat on the foot of Katie's bed.

Katie looked down at her tray. Toast, cut into little points, just the way she liked it. Grape jelly, the only kind she liked. And an egg. Soft-boiled. Just the way she liked it.

She smiled.

"Maybe it'll make you feel better," Mom said. "Chicken pox is mean, isn't it?"

Katie nodded. She took a bite of toast. She looked up at her mom. "You didn't believe me yesterday," she said. "I told you I was sick."

Mom made a sad face. "I'm sorry," she said. "I thought it was something else."

"Like what?" Katie said.

But then she looked away. She didn't want to know what. What if Mom knew that she was a thief?

"It doesn't last long, Katie," Mom said. "That's one good thing about it."

But it did last long, Katie thought. If you were a thief, that is. If you were a thief once, it probably meant you were a thief for good.

She sighed. She took another bite of toast, then pushed the tray away.

Baby-Child had crept to the side of the bed. Katie watched while he pulled himself up so he was standing. He was holding tight to the blankets with his fat little fingers. She could just see his fuzzy head over the side of the bed.

She leaned forward to him.

"What does the mother ducky say?" she asked him.

He grinned at her, showing all six of his teeth, four on the bottom and two on the top. "Quack!" he said, real loud.

Katie laughed.

"What does the baby ducky say?" Katie said.

"Quack!" Baby-Child said. "Quack, quack."

Katie patted his head. She liked it

when he said the word she had taught him.

She leaned back on her pillow and looked at her mom. "When's Grandpa getting here?" she said.

"Maybe by early afternoon," Mom said. "It's about a four-hour drive."

"Is Grandma coming, too?" Katie asked.

"Not this time," Mom said. "She had to work in the hospital gift shop today."

Katie nodded. She knew Grandma worked in the hospital gift shop. Grandma sold teddy bears to the daddies who had gotten new babies — well, she sold them to the daddies FOR the new babies. Katie thought that would be a fun job to have when she grew up.

"Grandpa wanted to bring you a gift, too," Mom said. "But I didn't know what you wanted."

Katie looked at her mom, wide-eyed. "What did you tell him?" she asked.

"Nothing," Mom said. "I didn't know what to tell him."

"Mo-om!" Katie said. "Why didn't you ask me?"

She could feel herself about to cry. She made a very mad face at her mom and opened her eyes wide. She didn't want her mom to know she felt like crying.

Mom shrugged. "Katie," she said, "I tried to ask you. I came upstairs right after you spoke to Grandpa. But you were already sound asleep."

The Pocahontas costume. She wanted the Pocahontas costume. She could feel tears come under her eyelids. Grandpa always brought good presents. But he didn't know.

Katie looked over at her clock. Eleven o'clock.

"Is it too late to call him now?" Katie said.

"I'm sure he left already," Mom said. "But don't worry. Obie told him what you wanted."

"He did?" Katie said. "What?"

Mom reached for Katie's tray. "Well," she said. "I think your grandpa spoils you entirely too much. But he said he'd get it." She smiled at Katie. "The Pocahontas costume."

Katie drew a deep breath and leaned back against her pillow.

The Pocahontas costume. She'd have a Pocahontas costume. Just like Tiffany. Just like Tawana. She could wear it to the Thanksgiving program. She'd have the dress. And the ballet slippers. And the . . .

She looked at her mom. "Is he bringing the whole thing?" she said. "Everything? The whole outfit?"

Mom shrugged. "I guess. I don't know what comes with it. Let's wait and see."

She picked up Katie's tray, then set it on the dresser.

"I'll be back in a minute," she said. "I'm going to start your bathwater. It will help the itching. Watch Baby-Child."

She went out of the room and closed the door.

Katie could hear the bathwater begin to run.

She lay back on her pillows and closed her eyes. She whispered over and over to herself.

"The beaded headband," she whispered. "Oh please, oh please, oh please."

15

A Visit
from Grandpa

Katie was so excited she could hardly stand it. She wanted to wait for Grandpa outside on the steps. That way, she could watch down the street and see his car coming.

But Mom said, "No way, young lady. You're sick already." So she ended up waiting for him in bed. And she fell sound asleep.

When she woke up, Grandpa was already there, sitting in the chair beside her bed, reading.

He looked at her over his glasses as she opened her eyes.

"Grandpa!" she said. "Hi." She reached out and patted his hand.

"Hi," Grandpa said. He leaned over and kissed her gently on her forehead.

"You got here," she said.

"I got here," he answered.

Katie sat up and stretched. She felt all sleepy-like.

She felt her face.

It was hot and itchy. And she could feel new hot spots on her forehead.

"Does it hurt?" Grandpa said.

Katie shook her head. "It itches," she said.

"Poor you," Grandpa said.

Katie shrugged. "It's okay."

"You awake now?" Grandpa asked. "Or do you want to go back to sleep awhile? I'll just sit here next to you."

"I'm awake now," Katie said.

"Want to play a game?" Grandpa said. "Or watch a video? I brought a new one."

"You did?" Katie said. She sat up straighter.

"Uh-huh," Grandpa said. "A present. A new video."

"A present?" Katie said.

Grandpa nodded.

"Oh," Katie said.

"A Pocahontas video," Grandpa said.

"Oh," Katie said again.

A Pocahontas video. But she wanted the costume!

She could feel tears creep up to her eyes again.

She was getting like Tiffany. Crybaby Tiffany!

"You're feeling really bad, aren't you?" Grandpa said.

She nodded and looked away.

Grandpa put a hand on her forehead. "You feel a little hot," he said.

"I'm okay," she said.

"Want to go downstairs and watch the video?" Grandpa said. "Or I could bring in the little TV and VCR from your mom's room."

Katie just shook her head again.

Grandpa reached over and took her hand. "Know what?" he said. "When I was little, I thought that chicken pox was called 'chicken spots.' I thought you got it from eating too much chicken."

Katie nodded.

"And then when someone told me it wasn't chicken spots from eating chicken, you know what I thought then?"

Katie didn't answer.

"I thought they were lying to me," Grandpa said. "For a long time after, I wouldn't eat any chicken. But I couldn't tell anyone why, what I was thinking."

Katie nodded. She knew about that. It happened to her a lot lately.

"Sure you don't want to see the video?" Grandpa said. "I thought *Pocahontas* was one of your favorites."

Katie just shrugged.

It was.

She sat up straighter. She didn't want Grandpa to feel bad. "Later," she said. "Okay?"

She swung her legs out of bed. "I have to go to the bathroom," she said.

Grandpa pushed the chair back and made room for her to get up. He handed her her slippers that were beside the bed. They were pink ones with bunny fur on them. Grandpa had brought them for her on his last visit.

Katie bent over to put them on.

And that's when she saw the box beside Grandpa on the floor. A big box. Much bigger than a video. It was in a bag from the Disney Store.

She looked up at Grandpa. "What's that?" she said.

Grandpa raised his eyebrows. "What's what?" he said.

Katie pointed. "That!"

Grandpa looked down to where Katie was pointing. "Well, I don't know," he said. He acted surprised. "I wonder."

Katie could tell that he was teasing. "You brought it!" she said.

"Well, maybe I did," he said. "What do you think it is?"

A Pocahontas costume, she hoped!

"A present?" she said.

Grandpa picked it up and handed it to her. "I think you'd better open it," he said.

"I think so, too," Katie said. She sat back down on the bed.

Grandpa helped her pull the box out of the bag.

She lifted the lid. It stuck, and she tugged at it.

Grandpa helped a little, and it came off with a *whoosh*.

Katie reached in. There was a lot of paper inside.

Her heart was pounding very, very hard.

Oh please, *oh please*, *oh please*, she prayed.

She pulled out the paper. She held her breath. She closed her eyes for just a second. She opened them.

And there it was. The Pocahontas costume. The absolutely beautiful Pocahontas costume. It was even more beautiful than she remembered Tiffany's was, even better. It was brown and soft with a scallopy bottom, like a real Native American girl's. It had a rope thing for a belt, a nice one.

She held it up to her, then buried her face in it. It even smelled nice.

She looked up at Grandpa and smiled.

Grandpa smiled back.

She turned around then and laid the dress on the bed.

She turned back to the box. There was more stuff.

She reached in — shoes. Beaded moccasins, like ballerina shoes. They were beautiful, brown, and as soft as slippers.

She held them to her face and sniffed at them, too. Leather, she loved the smell of leather. She put them on the bed, too.

She turned back to the box and pulled away the rest of the paper. There was a little bag tucked into a corner. She lifted it out.

She turned it upside down. She shook it.

Something fell out. A headband. A beaded headband. A wonderful, beautiful, beaded headband.

The little beads were shiny in the sun coming through her window.

Katie smiled and picked it up. She let her fingers run over the smooth beads.

She pictured how it would look on her. She pictured it on her hair, shining in the sun. She pictured herself as the real Pocahontas, dancing for her father, the chief.

She looked at the headband again.

She pictured it on Tiffany's head, on her long, straight hair.

She sighed.

Well, she had the costume. And the shoes.

She reached over and gave Grandpa a hug, a big hug. "It's perfect," she whispered. "Just what I wanted."

16

Back to School

It took more than a whole week before Katie was allowed to go back to school. Her chicken pox was even worse than Obie's. She had spots everywhere and she ran a fever and she itched.

She was very worried, because it was almost time for the Thanksgiving program. She had to be back to wear her Pocahontas costume. And to make things better with Tiffany.

And she was sad, because she was missing out on all the fun. Every day she asked Obie about it, and every day he told her what they were doing. He said they had smushed the cranberries and made cranberry sauce. He said they had made corn muffins. That took two whole days. That's because Emil had dropped the batter on the floor the first time, right before they were going to put it in the baking cups. So the next day, they had to start all over. But the corn muffins were finally made.

They had even made the butter. Bobby Bork had gotten to churn the butter — Katie's job. That made her even sadder.

Now all the food was made and stored in the cafeteria refrigerator, waiting for the program. Katie had missed it all.

Every day, Katie told Mom she was better. Every day Mom checked her for spots. And every day she had new ones.

But finally, one day there were no more new spots. Still, she had to wait another day and then another and then wait until all the old spots had scabs.

By the time she was allowed back, it

was the very last day before Thanksgiving. It was the morning of the breakfast and the program.

Katie could hardly wait to get to school. She never knew she'd miss it so much. That morning, she was up early. She put on her Pocahontas outfit — the dress and the belt and the moccasins. But not the headband.

She looked at herself in the mirror. She turned this way and that way. She twirled around. She was an American Indian princess. She was dancing for the chief.

She was beautiful.

She ran into Obie's room.

Obie was sitting on the floor, trying to get a knot out of his sneakers. He looked up at her.

"Look!" Katie said. "Don't I look beautiful?"

She threw her arms out and twirled around.

Obie nodded. "Like an Indian princess," he said.

Katie smiled at him.

He was wearing an Indian headpiece made out of construction paper. Some of the feathers were drooping over his forehead.

"You look nice, too, Obie," Katie said. "I like your feathers."

Obie stood up. He pushed the feathers out of his eyes and looked at his watch.

"Hurry," he said.

Katie went back to her room and got her school things. She got her coat and her backpack. She got the headband.

Then she went over and looked in the mirror once more. She leaned in close. She took the headband and slid it onto her head. She put it across her forehead like an Indian princess.

She turned this way and that way in the light.

Beautiful. It was beautiful.

She sighed.

She took it off and stuck it into her backpack again.

She wished she could keep it. But she couldn't. She had a plan for it. And hoped like anything that this time it would work.

17

Thankful Katie

At school, everyone was all excited. The mothers and fathers were coming in a little while, and all the breakfast things had been set out in the cafeteria.

Mrs. Henry gave Katie a big hug to welcome her back.

But she pretended not to recognize her. "Who is this beautiful Native American girl?" she said, holding Katie away from her.

"You know who I am!" Katie said.

Mrs. Henry frowned. "Well, I think I recognize that voice," she said, slowly.

Katie laughed. "It's me!" she said. "Katie! And I'm all better."

"I'm glad," Mrs. Henry said, and gave her another hug.

Katie went to her desk then. She still had her coat on. She waited until everyone else was finished in the coat closet. Then she went to put her coat away.

Nobody in there.

She looked all around her. Absolutely nobody.

She hung up her coat. She bent down. She put the headband in a safe place. A really, really safe place. And then she hurried back to her seat.

All the kids were sitting down. But they were all still talking and looking at each other's costumes. All the boys were either Pilgrim boys or American Indians, and the girls were Pilgrim girls or American Indian girls. Some of the boys and some of the girls wore feathers in their hair. Amelia's hair was braided like an Indian girl's and she had a feather stuck over one ear. Katie wished she had thought of asking Mom to braid her hair.

She smiled at Amelia. "You look nice," she said.

"So do you," Amelia said. "I'm glad you're back."

"Me, too," Katie said. She slid into her seat. She looked over at Tiffany.

Tiffany was dressed just like Katie — exact same dress. Exact same shoes.

And neither of them had a headband.

Tiffany saw Katie looking at her.

Tiffany made a big fat breath.

Katie frowned. But she said, "You look nice."

Tiffany made a frowny face, too. She looked down at her fingernails. "So do you," she said.

"I like your dress," Katie said.

Tiffany nodded. "And my shoes," she said.

She stuck out her feet so Katie could see.

Katie stuck out her feet, too.

"You don't have a headband," Tiffany said.

Katie just shrugged. She could feel her heart beat sort of hard. "I did," she said. "But I . . . gave it away."

"How come?" Tiffany said.

Katie shrugged. "My baby — sister — wanted it," she said.

She thought Baby-Child wouldn't mind being turned into a girl for now.

"Oh," Tiffany said.

"I know where yours is, though," Katie said.

Tiffany just rolled her eyes.

"I do," Katie said.

"Boys and girls?" Mrs. Henry said. "Pay attention, now. We need to take attendance and go over everything one more time. Our families will be here in no time."

Tiffany leaned over to Katie's desk. "Where?" she whispered.

Katie made her shoulders go up. "Right where you left it," she said.

"Katie?" Mrs. Henry said. "Tiffany? Are you paying attention?"

Katie didn't look up. But she nodded.

"All right then," Mrs. Henry said. "I'm going to call the roll, and when I do, I want each person to say their lines from the program. All right?"

Everybody got very still.

Everybody but Tiffany.

She leaned closer to Katie. "Where?" she said.

Katie looked up at Mrs. Henry. Mrs. Henry was calling on Emil.

Emil had a little tiny voice. Mrs. Henry was saying his lines with him, trying to get him to say them louder.

Katie leaned close to Tiffany. "In the coat closet, probably," she whispered. "Something's in your cubby. I saw it."

Tiffany stood up. She didn't even ask to be excused. She hurried into the coat closet.

Mrs. Henry didn't seem to notice.

Mrs. Henry called on Katie next.

Katie had been practicing, even when she was home sick.

She said:

"The people worked and built a ship, the *Mayflower*, to take them on a trip across the Atlantic."

"Very good, Katie," Mrs. Henry said. She smiled.

She called Maria's name next.

Maria said, "A bright and graceful child am I, about nine years of age, and I will change the course of history."

Katie turned and looked at her.

Maria was dressed in a Native American–type dress, too, but not like Katie's or Tiffany's. It was tan and looked like it was made of silk. It was beautiful. Katie noticed that Maria wasn't frowning anymore, either.

Katie smiled at Maria.

"You look beautiful," Katie whispered to her.

Maria smiled back.

Mrs. Henry called Tiffany's name.

Tiffany had just slid back into her seat.

Katie could see her clutching something in her hand.

"We share our bounty and our goods," Tiffany said. Her voice came out all breathless-like. "We call you friend; you call us friend."

"Very good, Tiffany," Mrs. Henry said. "But slow down, all right?"

Tiffany nodded.

Next Mrs. Henry called on Bobby Bork.

Katie looked at Tiffany then. Tiffany opened her hand. Katie saw the headband lying there.

"I found it!" Tiffany whispered.

Katie didn't answer. She just watched as Tiffany stretched the headband out and slid it onto her hair — Katie's beautiful beaded headband. It hugged Tiffany's forehead and head just right.

Tiffany turned to Katie, smiling.

It wasn't a mean smile, just a happy one. She fluffed out her hair. She tossed her head. She turned to the front and sat up straight and tall. She touched the headband. She looked very happy.

Katie tossed her head. She sat up straight and tall. She thought she was happy, too.

Mrs. Henry called Obie's name then and he said his lines. He said them good and loud.

Katie had heard them a million times when he practiced at home. But in her head, she said them with him.

The wee bird sings and greets the morn.

The birdlings wake and peep.

We thank thee for the birdlings small.

We thank the Lord for all.

Katie took a deep breath. She smiled at Obie.

She thought that was exactly right, exactly how she felt. Thankful for her home and her parents and her grandpa and Obie.

Thankful for Sam and Matt and Baby-Child.

Thankful that she wasn't a thief.

She snuck a look at Tiffany.

And she couldn't help thinking the headband would look better on her own hair.

LITTLE 🍎 APPLE®

*T*here are fun times ahead with kids just like you in Little Apple books! Once you take a bite out of a Little Apple—you'll want to read more!

Reading Excitement for Kids with BIG Appetites!

Have You Read Our Latest Adventure?

The Adventures of
MARY-KATE & ASHLEY™

Help Us Solve Any Crime By Dinner Time!™

☑ BBO86369-X	#1: *The Case of the Sea World® Adventure*	$3.99
☐ BBO86370-3	#2: *The Case of the Mystery Cruise™*	$3.99
☐ BBO86231-6	#3: *The Case of the Fun House Mystery*	$3.99
☑ BBO88008-1	#4: *The Case of the U.S. Space Camp® Mission™*	$3.99

Available wherever you buy books, or use this order form.
Scholastic Inc., P.O. Box 7502, 2931 E. McCarty Street, Jefferson City, MO 65102

Please send me the books I have checked above. I am enclosing $_____
(please add $2.00 to cover shipping and handling).
Send check or money order – no cash or C.O.D.s please.

Name Devin Zeigler   Birthdate April 6th

Address 10912 Cody Lane

City Fishers In.   State /Zip 46038

Please allow four to six weeks for delivery. Offer good in U.S.A. only. Sorry, mail orders are not available to residents to Canada. Prices subject to change.